TEN OF THE BEST MYTHS,
LEGENDS & FOLK STORIES

TEN OF THE BEST
MYTHICAL HERO
STORIES

DAVID WEST

Crabtree Publishing Company
www.crabtreebooks.com

Crabtree Publishing Company
www.crabtreebooks.com
1-800-387-7650

Publishing in Canada
616 Welland Ave.
St. Catharines, ON
L2M 5V6

Published in the United States
PMB 59051, 350 Fifth Ave.
59th Floor,
New York, NY

Published in **2015 by CRABTREE PUBLISHING COMPANY.**

Printed in the U.S.A./092014/JA20140811

Created and produced by:
David West Children's Books

Project development, design, and concept:
David West Children's Books

Author and designer: David West

Illustrator: David West

Contributing Editor: Steve Parker

Editor: Anastasia Suen

Proofreader: Wendy Scavuzzo

Production coordinator and Prepress technicians:
Samara Parent, Margaret Amy Salter

Print coordinator: Katherine Berti

Library and Archives Canada Cataloguing in Publication

West, David, 1956-, author
    Ten of the best mythical hero stories / David West.

(Ten of the best : myths, legends & folk stories)
Includes index.
Issued in print and electronic formats.
ISBN 978-0-7787-0785-1 (bound).--ISBN 978-0-7787-1063-9 (pbk.).--
ISBN 978-1-4271-7745-2 (pdf).--ISBN 978-1-4271-7737-7 (html)

    1. Tales. I. Title. II. Title: Mythical hero stories.

PZ8.1.W37My 2014   j398.21   C2014-903858-5
                                             C2014-903859-3

Library of Congress Cataloging-in-Publication Data

West, David, 1956-
Ten of the best mythical hero stories / David West.
    pages cm -- (Ten of the best: myths, legends & folk stories)
Includes index.
 ISBN 978-0-7787-0785-1 (reinforced library binding) --
ISBN 978-0-7787-1063-9 (pbk.) --
ISBN 978-1-4271-7745-2 (electronic pdf) --
ISBN 978-1-4271-7737-7 (electronic html)
1. Mythology--Juvenile literature. 2. Heroes--Juvenile literature. 3. Legends--Juvenile literature. I. Title.

BL312.W47 2015
398.22--dc23
                            2014022868

THE STORIES

Theseus

Theseus, one of ancient Greece's greatest heroes, was son of Aegeus the King of Athens.

Every seven years, Athens had to send seven young women and seven young men as a tribute to King Minos of Crete. They were to be devoured by the Minotaur. This horrific beast, half man and half bull, lived in a maze, or labyrinth, made by a man called Daedalus.

The third time, Theseus asked to take the place of one young man – and slay the monster. He told his father Aegeus that his returning ship would display white sails to show his success.

When Theseus arrived in Crete, King Minos's daughter Ariadne fell in love with him at first sight. Before the Athenians were sent into the labyrinth, she secretly passed to Theseus a sword and ball of wool.

The labyrinth, a maze of tunnels, was under King Minos's Palace of Knossos. Legend said that no one could find a way out.

Bulls and bull worship were important in Minoan Crete. Acrobats leaping over bulls were part of their religious rituals.

Theseus tied one end of the wool at the entrance to the labyrinth. He unraveled it and would later be able to find his way back. As he set off into the maze, the Minotaur's terrible roar echoed through the tunnels.

Theseus finally arrived at the beast's lair, which was strewn with human bones. Suddenly, the monstrous form of the Minotaur appeared. Seeing Theseus, it let out a blood-curdling bellow, lowered its head, and charged. Brave Theseus stood firm and, with one swift blow of the sword given to him by Ariadne, he killed the monster.

Theseus and the Athenian youths escaped. They fled from Crete, taking Ariadne with them.

But, on his return, the hero forgot to raise white sails instead of black ones. His father saw the returning ship. Believing Theseus to be dead, Aegeus threw himself from the cliffs into the sea – the Aegean Sea.

Perseus

The ancient Greek hero Perseus was the son of Zeus, king of gods, and Danae, the daughter of King Acrisius of Argos.

King Acrisius was told he would be killed by his daughter's son. So he cast his daughter Danae and her son Perseus into the sea in a chest. Washed up on the Isle of Seriphos, they were cared for by the fisherman Dictys.

Dictys raised Perseus as his own son. Dictys's brother Polydectes was king of the Isle of Seriphos and wanted to marry beautiful Danae. But she had no interest in him, and her son Perseus protected her from his attentions.

One day, the king tricked Perseus into promising him any gift. Polydectes asked for the head of the Gorgon Medusa, whose stare turned people to stone. As Perseus set off on this quest, Polydectes thought he had finally rid himself of the troublesome son of the woman he loved.

The goddess **Athena** was alarmed. She instructed Perseus to find the **Hesperides** nymphs, who had weapons to defeat the Gorgon. First Perseus had to find the Graeae—three old women with one eye between them—because they knew the location of the Hesperides' garden. The Graeae revealed this only when Perseus snatched away their eye. Upon finding the Hesperides, Perseus received weapons and a polished shield.

At last, Perseus arrived at the Gorgon's lair. As he picked his way through the stone statues of Medusa's lifeless victims, he heard a slithering noise behind him. Using the polished shield as a mirror, he saw the Gorgon about to strike. Closing his eyes, he turned around and slashed out with his sword – cutting off her head.

Perseus returned to Seriphos for his revenge. Polydectes watched him arrive. The hero held up Medusa's head and the king looked at it. He turned to stone.

Perseus eventually gave Medusa's head to Athena, who had it mounted on Zeus's shield.

Heracles

Heracles, also called Hercules by the Romans, was the greatest of the ancient Greek heroes. His father was Zeus and his mother was Alcmene, a mortal (human).

Zeus's wife, the goddess Hera, hated Heracles, who was not her son. One day she made Heracles so angry that he killed his wife and children. As punishment, Heracles's arch-enemy King Eurystheus gave him twelve difficult tasks, called labors.

Heracles was only eight months old when Hera sent two giant snakes into his room. Heracles showed no fear. He grabbed a snake in each hand and strangled them.

Heracles's first labor was to kill the Nemean Lion and bring back its skin. Using his immense strength, he managed to strangle the lion. But he had difficulty skinning it, since nothing could penetrate its hide. Eventually the goddess Athena advised him to use one of the lion's own claws. Heracles returned wearing the lion's skin. King Eurystheus was so afraid, he hid in a large storage jar.

Heracles's second labor was to kill the Lernaean Hydra. This many-headed serpent lived in swampy Lake Lerna. It had poisonous breath, and its blood killed anyone it touched.

Upon reaching Lerna, Heracles attacked the beast, knocking off one of its many heads. To his dismay, he discovered that each time he removed a head, two grew back in its place.

Heracles asked his nephew Iolaus to help him. Iolaus suggested using a firebrand to scorch and seal the neck stumps each time a head was cut off – and the second labor was achieved.

Eventually, Heracles managed to complete all twelve of his labors.

Heracles' Twelve Labors
1. *Kill and skin the Nemean Lion.*
2. *Destroy the Lernaean Hydra.*
3. *Capture the Golden Hind of Artemis.*
4. *Capture the Erymanthian Boar.*
5. *Clean the Augean Stables in a single day.*
6. *Slay the Stymphalian Birds.*
7. *Capture the Cretan Bull.*
8. *Steal the Mares of Diomedes.*
9. *Steal the belt of Amazon queen Hippolyte.*
10. *Steal the cattle of the giant Geryon.*
11. *Steal the golden apples of the Hesperides.*
12. *Capture and bring back Cerberus.*

Horatius

Horatius Cocles was an officer in the army of the ancient Roman Republic. It was the time when the army of Lars Porsena, King of Clusium, attacked the City of Rome.

As Porsena's army approached Rome, country people fled to the safety of the city. Its walls and the River Tiber provided formidable defense. Only one wooden bridge allowed access to the city across the Tiber. This was guarded by soldiers under the command of Horatius Cocles.

The panic of the fleeing people spread to Horatius's soldiers, who threw down their weapons and ran. Realizing the importance of the bridge, Horatius tried to stop his men running away. But only two brave soldiers stayed with him.

Lars Porsena was an Etruscan king known for his war against the City of Rome. The Etruscans were a civilization of ancient Italy, which eventually became part of the Roman Republic in the late 4th century BCE.

Horatius shouted to the fleeing soldiers to fetch axes and destroy the bridge behind him, while he and his two loyal companions held back the enemy.

The Etruscan soldiers attacked. The three Romans fought bravely to keep them at bay. A shout eventually came from the Roman soldiers behind: "The bridge is about to collapse!"

Horatius told his two companions to go while he continued to repel the enemy. As the Etruscans attacked again, Horatius was wounded several times. Then a portion of the bridge gave way. Knowing that the city was now safe, Horatius jumped into the River Tiber. Although wounded, and wearing heavy armor, this hero of Rome managed to swim to safety.

Lars Porsena's army attacked Rome. One night, a Roman youth named Gaius Mucius sneaked into the Etruscan camp to kill Porsena, but killed his secretary by mistake. When captured, Mucius said that he was just the first of 300 youths to attempt this feat – and thrust his hand into a fire. Porsena was so impressed, he quickly made a peace treaty with Rome.

Beowulf

Beowulf was a heroic warrior of the Scandinavian people called the Geats, during the late 5th century CE.

Beowulf and his men were asleep in the great hall at Heorot. They had spent most of the night drinking and singing with their host Hrothgar, king of the **Danes**. But out in the dark, their noise tormented the giant beast Grendel. It entered the great hall to destroy the noise-makers.

The Geats were a tribe that lived in Gotland, Sweden. The story of Beowulf survives as a manuscript, written in the 8th century CE by an Anglo-Saxon poet in England.

The screams of one warrior being ripped apart by Grendel woke the rest of the men. Beowulf sprang to his feet and attacked the monster and tore off one of its arms. Grendel ran howling into the night.

The king and his men rejoiced, but not for long. Soon a more terrifying creature attacked the hall, killing another trusted warrior. It was Grendel's mother, come to avenge her son's death. As she left, Beowulf tracked her to her lair in a lake.

Diving into the lake, Beowulf battled the monster. But his sword broke on her back and only his well-made armor saved him from her fury. With luck, at the bottom of the lake was a mighty sword. Beowulf seized it and struck off his foe's head. Beowulf was honored as a hero and made king of the Geats.

Fifty years later, a golden cup was stolen from a dragon's lair. The dragon terrified the country, burning the land. Beowulf, now an old man, faced the dragon with one warrior, Wiglaf. Together they killed the dragon, but Beowulf was badly wounded. He died and was buried along with the dragon's treasure.

The Mayan Hero Twins

The hero twins Hunahpu and Xbalanque were summoned to the Mayan underworld, called Xibalba, by the lords who dwelled there.

The hero twins' father and uncle were famed ball-players, but they were lured to the underworld and killed by the Lords of Xibalba.

The Mayan civilization existed in Central America from 2000 BCE to 900 CE. Temples and other stone buildings are still being discovered in the jungle today.

Later, the hero twins Hunahpu and Xbalanque caught a rat. It bargained for its life by telling them how their father and uncle had been tricked and where to find their ball-playing gear. Finding the ball-playing equipment, they released the rat and decided to have a game themselves. But the noise they made upset the Lords of Xibalba. And so the twins were summoned to the underworld for a ball game there.

Knowing how their father and uncle had been tricked and killed, the twins were ready to avenge their deaths. The journey to the underworld was difficult and dangerous, but eventually they arrived.

Hunahpu and Xbalanque were met by the Lords of Xibalba, who gave them several tests. The twins passed the tests easily – which angered the Lords. Eventually they all played a ball game. The twins beat the Lords at that, too, which made the Lords even angrier.

Played in a special court by hitting a rubber ball through a stone ring, ball games were a Mayan way of settling disputes and even wars.

Knowing the Lords would never set them free again, Hunahpu and Xbalanque allowed themselves to be burned alive. But when their ashes were scattered in a river, the twins were revived. At first they became fish, then they became human.

Now the heroes had great magic. They could kill people, then bring them back to life! The Lords of Xibalba heard of this feat. They summoned the twins back to the underworld to perform this magic on them.

The Lords of Xibalba allowed the hero twins to kill them. But the twins got their revenge – they did no magic and left the Lords in the underworld.

Jason

Jason was an ancient Greek hero, famous as the leader of the Argonauts on their quest for the Golden Fleece. His father was Aison, the rightful king of Iolcos.

Jason agreed to undertake a quest for the Golden Fleece. He knew that if he succeeded, the throne of Iolcos would be his. He gathered 50 men and set sail in the ship **Argo**. Jason and his men, the Argonauts, had many adventures before they arrived at Colchis, the home of the Golden Fleece. The fleece was owned by King Aietes and guarded by a never-sleeping dragon.

Jason left his men on the *Argo* and met with Aietes alone. Aietes promised to give the fleece to Jason, but only if he could perform three tasks. The tasks were difficult and Jason was discouraged.

*The goddess Hera persuaded the goddess Aphrodite to help Jason. Aphrodite convinced her son **Eros** to make Aietes's daughter Medea fall in love with Jason so that she would help him.*

With the gods' help, the sorceress Medea – Aietes's daughter – fell in love with Jason. She used her magic to help him complete the three tasks. First, Jason had to plow a field with fire-breathing oxen. But he was protected from the oxen's flames by an ointment that Medea had given him.

Second, Jason was to sow dragon's teeth in the field. These quickly sprouted into an army of skeleton warriors, ready to attack him. Jason threw a rock at one, as Medea had told him. The warrior, thinking another warrior had struck him, hit out. Soon the warriors were fighting each other. Not one was left standing.

The third task was to overcome the waking dragon. Medea had given Jason a magic potion to make the dragon sleep. As the dragon dozed off, Jason grabbed the Golden Fleece. With Medea, he headed back to the *Argo* and his men.

Jason had accomplished the seemingly impossible quest for the Golden Fleece. But there were still many dangers to face before he could claim his rightful place as king of Iolcos.

Rustam

*The ancient Persian hero Rustam is famed for his Seven Trials. They occurred on a journey to save his **Shah**, Kay Kavus, who was captured by demons.*

On their epic journey, Rustam and his brave horse Rakhsh fought lions, dragons, demons, and almost died of thirst in a desert.

Eventually, Rustam arrived at Mazinderan, where the Shah and his army were held. They had been blinded by an evil spell and were guarded by Mazinderan's demon chief, Arzang. In a fierce fight, Rustam killed the Mazinderan champion, Olad. Before Olad died, he told Rustam where Arzang hid.

Persia, modern-day Iran, has had several powerful empires. The first, founded in the 6th century BCE by Cyrus the Great, spanned parts of Europe, Africa and Asia. It was eventually conquered by Alexander the Great in 330 BCE.

Rustam defeated Arzang in fierce combat, then returned to Mazinderan to free the Shah and his men. But he discovered that they were blind. From the Shah, Rustam learned that the White Demon had cast the spell of no sight. And it was only the blood of the demon's heart that could lift the curse.

Rustam rode to the White Demon's lair and bellowed his name. From a cave the giant demon attacked, roaring and snarling. But Rustam was too quick and strong. With a mighty blow, the hero struck down the demon, cut out its heart, then returned to the Shah and his men. There the demon's blood cured the spell. Some say Rustam also cut off the demon's head and wore its skull as a helmet!

Sinbad

Sinbad was a mythical sailor and hero based in the port of Basrah, southern Iraq, around the end of the 6th century CE. Stories of his seven voyages are filled with magical places and monsters. This is the tale of his second voyage.

Sinbad grew restless with his life ashore and set off on a second voyage. Through clever trading, he had made a small fortune and headed home. His ship stopped at a deserted island to replenish stores. Taking wine and food onto the beach, Sinbad stretched his legs. As he rested beneath a tree, he soon fell asleep.

When Sinbad awoke he found, with rising panic, that the ship had gone. He had been abandoned! Climbing a tree to survey the land, he saw a distant white object and made his way toward it. The object turned out to be a giant egg that measured at least fifty paces around.

Ports in the Middle East were full of travelers and sailors with stories and tales about the Far East.

Suddenly a monstrous bird – a roc – landed and nestled over the egg. Sinbad hid in its shadow. Quickly realizing that the bird was his way off the island, he used his turban to tie himself to its leg.

As Sinbad hoped, in the morning, the roc took off and carried him a great distance. Eventually they landed in a valley of giant snakes. As Sinbad untied himself, the roc attacked a snake and carried it away. Looking around, to his great surprise Sinbad saw the ground was covered with giant gemstones!

Sinbad spent the day collecting as many gems as he could carry. He was little troubled by the snakes, who hid in caves, away from the rocs.

Suddenly a large slab of meat landed nearby! Sinbad remembered stories of how merchants threw lumps of meat over the valley's cliff, hoping gemstones would stick to them. The rocs grabbed the meat and took it to their nests. When the birds flew off, the merchants seized the gems.

Sinbad tied himself and his gems to the largest piece of meat and lay underneath. Presently a roc arrived and carried the meat to its nest. In that way, Sinbad was rescued by merchants and their ship. He returned home with a vast fortune in gems.

William Tell

William Tell was a folk hero of Switzerland during the early 14th century. He was famous for his skill with a crossbow.

Many years ago, the people of Switzerland were ruled by a cruel tyrant named Gessler. One day, he had a tall pole erected in the town square of Altdorf. At the top, was placed his hat. Gessler ordered that all those who passed by should bow to his hat.

But one man from the countryside, William Tell, refused to bow. When Gessler heard this, he became angry.

"Soon the whole country will follow his example and, be sure, rebellion will follow," he reasoned. Gessler sent out a decree for William Tell's arrest.

When William Tell and his son next visited Altdorf, he was brought before Gessler. Fame of Tell's skill with the crossbow had reached Gessler's ears and so the tyrant devised a cruel plan. He ordered Tell's son to stand in the square with an apple on his head.

The crossbow was a weapon used by soldiers and hunters during medieval times. It fired a bolt that looked like a short, thick arrow.

"Shoot the apple from your son's head and you may go free," smiled Gessler. Tell said: "Will you make me kill my son?"

"Silence! You must hit the apple with one bolt. If you fail to shoot, my soldiers will kill the boy."

The son, with faith in his father's skill, stood firm. Tell fitted a bolt, took aim, and fired. The missile hit the apple, knocking it from his son's head. The people shouted with joy. But as Tell turned away, a bolt hidden in his clothing fell to the ground.

Gessler cried out, "What did you intend on doing with that?"

Tell replied: "Tyrant! Had I hurt my son, this bolt was yours."

It is said that much later, Tell shot and killed Gessler, and set his country free.

GLOSSARY

Argo The ship on which Jason and the Argonauts sailed, named after its builder, Argus

Athena The ancient Greek goddess of wisdom, courage, and handicrafts

Danes People who live in the Scandinavian country of Denmark

Eros The ancient Greek god of love, who can make a person fall in love with whomever he chooses

Hesperides Nymphs who tend a blissful garden in a far western corner of the ancient mythical world

Shah Iranian name for king or ruler

INDEX